WHOMPERS

AND

WHAMMIES

For my mother

First Edition   1 2 3 4 5 6 7 8 9 10

Library of Congress Cataloging in Publication Data
Stern, Peter. Whompers and whammies : the great
circus war / by Peter Stern.
     p.   cm.   Summary: A misunderstanding creates a
feud between two talented families of trapeze artists.
ISBN 0-688-10775-3. — ISBN 0-688-10776-1 (lib. bdg.)
[1. Aerialists—Fiction. 2. Circus—Fiction. 3. Vendetta—
Fiction.] I. Title. PZ7.S83894Wh 1993 [E]—dc20
91-26083 CIP AC

PETER STERN

WHOMPERS
AND
WHAMMIES

 THE GREAT CIRCUS WAR

Lothrop, Lee & Shepard Books   New York

Jacques Streeber was the most daring high trapezer in the world. He was sure of it—nobody else had
ever done the Reverse Grand Boom Boom. His family,
the Soaring Streebers, all agreed he was Number One.

Oscar Zelwin, the Magnificent, thought *he* was king of the high trapeze. His claim to fame was the Double Whammy Supreme. To his family, the Flying Zelwins, he was tops.

If these two greats had never met, things would have been fine. But Fate plunked them down in the very same circus, *The Feeney Brothers' Colossal Spectacular.* The Feeneys chased back and forth all day trying to keep their stars happy. If Oscar wanted a new costume, a new costume was delivered to Jacques with the exact same number of sequins.

Although the program said "Soaring Streebers" first, it said "Flying Zelwins" bigger.

Each family lived in a fine circus car with built-in swings—one painted gold with silver trim, the other silver with gold. They even did their acts at exactly the same time and were announced by two ringmasters.

Jacques, over ring one, began by tossing off a
One-and-a-Half, bringing ahhhs from the crowd.
Over ring three, Oscar launched into a Backward
Cannonball. Gasps. Then Jacques threw a Flying
Whomper. Cheers. And, as the band tooted up, Oscar
hurled himself into an Over-Under-Ankle-Kiss.
Then, for the big finish—to a deafening drum roll—

Jacques did his Reverse Grand Boom Boom at the same moment as Oscar turned his Double Whammy Supreme. The crowd was on its feet.

Backstage, Oscar and Jacques bowed when they passed each other, saying things like "Fine crowd," and "Nice Whammy." That is, they did until the April night in Tashkent when the bottom dropped out.

Just as Jacques was twisting into his Flying Whomper, Oscar spotted something far below. Ferna, the Sacred White Elephant of Burma, a big high-trapeze fan, was sitting back to watch. But she was about to sit back *on* Toto, the World's Tiniest Grandfather. She didn't even see him. So Oscar yelled, "Watch it, kid!" Toto jumped.

The problem was—so did Jacques.
In midair. He vaulted right over the
outstretched hands of his brother
Ludlow and dropped two hundred
and forty-six feet onto his chin.
He smacked down so hard that
he bounced all the way back
up again, smiling and posing
as if it were all a great trick.

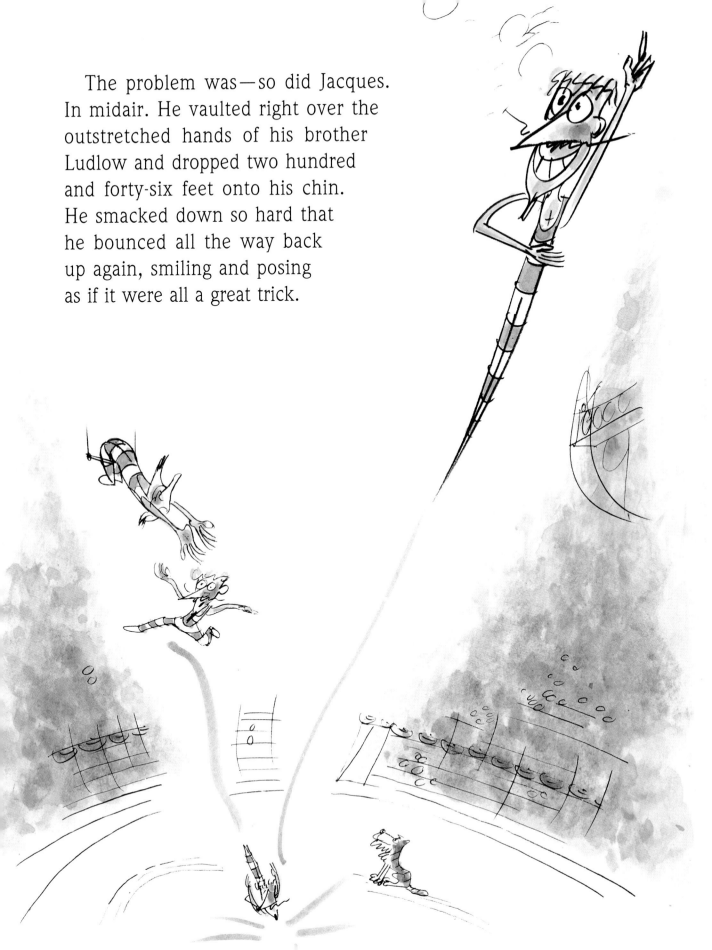

But he was furious. Oscar had ruined his act, and made him, Jacques Streeber, look like a rubber ball!

He started yelling even as Oscar somersaulted over: "From this day forth, you are to me *dirt*!"

Oscar wanted to apologize, but Jacques didn't give him a chance.

"Soot you are! Bugs!"

"But—" tried Oscar.

"Lima beans are better than you!"

This was too much. "You dare say this to me?"

"I dare?" said Jacques. "I do! Sure. And worse if I could think of it."

"Oh."

"Oh. Oh."

The Feeneys finally separated them. But the war was on.

Oscar forbade any Zelwin from talking to any Streeber. And Jacques forbade the other way. They even moved their cars to opposite ends of the train —Jacques up in front of the engine, Oscar behind the caboose.

The whole show took sides. The clowns, elephants, and horseback-riding poodles backed Oscar, while the lions and tigers, jugglers, and shoulder somersaulters stood by Jacques. (Benny, the Two-Headed Man, tried to get along with everybody, but each group only talked to one head.)

Rivalry filled the air. When Jacques showed off
The Youngest Streeber, Bobo, aged two, to the oohs
and ahhhs of the crowd, Oscar didn't rest until he
could, some months later, present Tina and Tappy,
The Amazing Baby Zelwin Twins. When Jacques did
a Double, Oscar pulled off a Triple. Then Jacques
astonished everyone with a Quadruple. Nobody ever

saw such tricks before. Nobody saw them too well
now, either, because the high trapeze had become
a battlefield.

Instead of waiting his turn, Oscar did his Cannonball right in the middle of Jacques's Whomper.
And Jacques launched his Boom Boom at the most
exciting moment of Oscar's Whammy.

It went on like this for quite a while. Years. So long that nobody could remember when Streebers and Zelwins got along. It might still be going on if there hadn't been that terrible dust storm in Minsk.

Everyone was coughing. Up on the high trapeze, a fit shook young Tappy Zelwin, one of the twins, now grown into a handsome man. He was about

to do a Sextuple when a great cough shot his
glasses right off. He froze. Without his glasses Tappy
couldn't see nearby things at all. Only faraway
things. So, at that moment, he looked up and saw
something he hadn't seen for many years: A
Streeber. The lovely violet eyes of Bobo Streeber,
now a beautiful young woman.

Their eyes locked across the top of the circus tent, across the lights and the swings, across the twirling bodies of their families. It was like a telegraph wire was strung between them and L-O-V-E flashed back and forth on the line.

After that, nothing was the same.

"You what?" yelled Oscar the next morning when Tappy told him the happy news. "You've fallen in love with the daughter of that sootball, Streeber?"

"Yes, I have, Father." Tappy smiled. "And we're going to be together always."

"Then you're going to be together somewhere

else from here. Because, from this moment on—"
Oscar's voice dropped very quiet.

"Oh, no!" cried Mother Zelwin.

"—you're a Flying Zelwin no longer!"

Tappy gulped, then bravely squared his shoulders and bade his family farewell.

"It must be my ears. I didn't hear this too right, eh?" Jacques Streeber asked his pride and joy, Bobo.

"No, I think you've got it, Father." She smiled. "I love Tappy."

"Oh, no!" "Oh, my!" "Oooh-la-la!" cried assorted Streebers in horror.

"So!" bellowed Jacques. "Aha! Then it is a Soaring Streeber you are no more!" And with that the great trapezer backflipped out the door.

"Ay-yi-yi," said the Feeneys when they heard the news.

Ta-dum-dum-dummy, ta-dum-dum-dumm, the drummer drummed several nights later in Allentown.

LADIES AND GENTLEMEN…
LADIES AND GENTLEMEN…
the two ringmasters shouted.
PREEESENTING…
PREEESENTING…
THE WORLD RENOWNED…
FABLED…
FANTASTIC…
UNBELIEVABLE…
AMAZING…
…FLYING ZELWINS!
…SOARING STREEBERS!

Half the band played a march for Oscar while the other half played a waltz for Jacques. Then it was Cannonballs, Reverse Boom Booms, and Double Whammies all at once.

Suddenly a hush fell over the tent. A third spotlight came on high over the center ring. There, two beaming figures sat on a swing—Tappy and Bobo. All they were doing was smiling and swinging, back and forth, back and forth. But they were such a happy sight that all eyes were upon them.

Jacques, twisting a Boom Boom, and Oscar, mid-Whammy, turned to look. Their mouths fell open. The breath caught in their throats. Their hearts raced. Then grins broke out across their faces. And, one by one, grins broke out across the faces of their families.

As a matter of fact, everyone in the whole circus tent—kids, elephants, poodles, jugglers, clowns, stilt walkers, Feeneys, Zelwins, and Streebers—were all grinning at once.

Then, before they even thought what they were doing, Oscar somersaulted over toward Jacques, and

Jacques toward Oscar, and in midair they gave each
other a hug. A HUG! Then another Streeber flipped
over and hugged another Zelwin, then another
and another, until the air surrounding Tappy and
Bobo was filled with twisting, grinning, hugging
trapezers.

Today, it's as if the trouble never happened. The two greats are together all the time. They teach now. Their prize pupil can do a Whammy and half a Boom Boom, and she's only seven months old. Her name is Theodora Streeber-Zelwin.

They say she's a natural.